A Note to Parents and Caregivers:

Read-it! Readers are for children who are just starting on the amazing road to reading. These beautiful books support both the acquisition of reading skills and the love of books.

 The PURPLE LEVEL presents basic topics and objects using high frequency words and simple language patterns.

 The RED LEVEL presents familiar topics using common words and repeating sentence patterns.

 The BLUE LEVEL presents new ideas using a larger vocabulary and varied sentence structure.

 The YELLOW LEVEL presents more challenging ideas, a broad vocabulary, and wide variety in sentence structure.

 The GREEN LEVEL presents more complex ideas, an extended vocabulary range, and expanded language structures.

 The ORANGE LEVEL presents a wide range of ideas and concepts using challenging vocabulary and complex language structures.

When sharing a book with your child, read in short stretches, pausing often to talk about the pictures. Have your child turn the pages and point to the pictures and familiar words. And be sure to reread favorite stories or parts of stories.

There is no right or wrong way to share books with children. Find time to read with your child, and pass on the legacy of literacy.

Adria F. Klein, Ph.D.
Professor Emeritus
California State University
San Bernardino, California

Editor: Jill Kalz
Designer: Tracy Davies
Page Production: Melissa Kes
Art Director: Nathan Gassman
The illustrations in this book were created with watercolor.

Picture Window Books
5115 Excelsior Boulevard
Suite 232
Minneapolis, MN 55416
877-845-8392
www.picturewindowbooks.com

Printed in the United States of America.

Library of Congress Cataloging-in-Publication Data
Jones, Christianne C.
Emma's new look / by Christianne C. Jones ; illustrated by Necdet Yilmaz.
p. cm. — (Read-it! readers)
Summary: Emma looks just like her father, but she wishes she did not, so each year
she tries a new look, until one day she realizes that looking like her father is not
necessarily a bad thing.
ISBN-13: 978-1-4048-3138-4 (library binding)
ISBN-10: 1-4048-3138-X (library binding)
ISBN-13: 978-1-4048-1230-7 (paperback)
ISBN-10: 1-4048-1230-X (paperback)
[1. Fathers and daughters—Fiction. 2. Individuality—Fiction. 3. Self-perception—
Fiction.] I. Yilmaz, Necdet, 1970– ill. II. Title.
PZ7.J6823Em 2006
[E]—dc22   2006027290

Emma's New Look

by Christianne C. Jones
illustrated by Necdet Yilmaz

Special thanks to our advisers for their expertise:

Adria F. Klein, Ph.D.
Professor Emeritus, California State University
San Bernardino, California

Susan Kesselring, M.A.
Literacy Educator
Rosemount–Apple Valley–Eagan (Minnesota) School District

PICTURE WINDOW BOOKS
Minneapolis, Minnesota

Everyone told Emma that she looked just like her dad.

Emma loved her dad, but she wanted her own look.

5

Emma didn't like her straight, dark hair or her brown eyes. She didn't like her nose or her smile.

"I don't want to look like Dad anymore. I need a new look," she told her mom.

In kindergarten, Emma wore striped socks and jeans every day. She put her hair in pigtails.

But she still looked like her dad.

In first grade, she wore a white T-shirt every day. She pulled her hair into a ponytail.

But she still looked like her dad.

In second grade, she wore a pink dress
and tights every day. She curled her hair.

But she still looked like her dad.

In third grade, she wore a warm-up suit every day. She tied her hair up with a white ribbon.

But she still looked like her dad.

In fourth grade, she wore red cowboy boots and glasses every day. She braided her hair.

But she still looked like her dad.

In fifth grade, she wore black every day.
She put her hair in a bun.

But she still looked like her dad.

In sixth grade, Emma had a new idea. She stopped trying to look different than her dad. She wore all of her favorite clothes. She wore her dark hair long and straight.

She still looked like her dad, but she didn't mind.

"I guess I'll always look like my dad, no matter what clothes I wear or what I do with my hair," Emma said.

"But that's OK. My dad is great. And together we make a wonderful team."

More *Read-it!* Readers

Bright pictures and fun stories help you practice your
reading skills. Look for more books at your level.

Benny and the Birthday Gift
The Best Lunch
The Boy Who Loved Trains
Car Shopping
Clinks the Robot
Firefly Summer
The Flying Fish
Gabe's Grocery List
Loop, Swoop, and Pull!
Marvin, the Blue Pig
Paulette's Friend
Pony Party
Princess Bella's Birthday Cake
The Princesses' Lucky Day
Rudy Helps Out
The Sand Witch
Say "Cheese"!
The Snow Dance
The Ticket
Tuckerbean in the Kitchen

Looking for a specific title or level? A complete list
of *Read-it!* Readers is available on our Web site:
www.picturewindowbooks.com